Caldecott Honor

Book

2012

Me...Jane

PATRICK McDONNELL

L **B**

LITTLE, BROWN AND COMPANY
NEW YORK   BOSTON

Jane Goodall's childhood drawings on pages 10 and 11, sketch on page 40, and photographs on pages 1, 38, and 39 appear courtesy of Jane Goodall.

Photograph on page 37 copyright © Hugo Van Lawick/National Geographic Stock, with permission from the National Geographic Society

Text and illustrations copyright © 2011 by Patrick McDonnell

Little, Brown and Company • Hachette Book Group • 237 Park Avenue, New York, NY 10017 • Visit our website at www.lb-kids.com

Little, Brown and Company is a division of Hachette Book Group, Inc. • The Little, Brown name and logo are trademarks of Hachette Book Group, Inc.

First Edition: April 2011

Library of Congress Cataloging-in-Publication Data: McDonnell, Patrick.   Me ... Jane / Patrick McDonnell. —1st ed.   p. cm.

Summary: Holding her stuffed toy chimpanzee, young Jane Goodall observes nature, reads Tarzan books, and dreams of living in Africa and helping animals.

Includes biographical information on the prominent zoologist.

ISBN 978-0-316-04546-9 1. Goodall, Jane, 1934- –Childhood and youth–Juvenile fiction. [1. Goodall, Jane, 1934- –Childhood and youth–Fiction. 2. Nature study–Fiction. 3. Toys–Fiction.] I. Title.

PZ7.M478443Me 2011   [Fic]–dc22   2010019756

10 9 8 7 6   WOR   Printed in the United States of America

The art for this book was done in India ink and watercolor on paper. The text was set in Caslon Book, and the display type is P22 Franklin Caslon.

Book layout by Jeff Schulz / Command-Z Design

Jane had a stuffed toy chimpanzee
named Jubilee.

She cherished Jubilee
and took him everywhere she went.

And Jane loved to be outside.

She watched birds making their nests,
spiders spinning their webs,
and squirrels chasing one another
up and down trees.

Jane learned all that she could about the animals
and plants she studied in her backyard
and read about in books.

THE ALIGATOR SOCIETY.

"WILD BIRD" PUZZLE

JUMBLED BIRD PUZZLE

1. WRINEGD.
2. HBLUFNILC.
3. DERWOKEOCP.
4. CNOLAF.
5. RWRSOAP.
6. FPINFU.

When you have put these in their
order you...

THE ALIGATOR

16. Pterodactyle

17. Eagle

COBRA'S PAGE.

COBRA'S ALIGATOR KNOWLEDGE.

1. What to mice eat?
2. What do cows eat?
3. What is a baby dog called?
4. What is a baby cat called?
5. What is a baby horse called?
6. What is a baby hen called.
7. Where does the egg that you eat for breakfast come from.
8. Tell me the names of 5 animals with tails.

COBRA'S DOTTING COMPETITION.

Here is something to pass the time away, Cobra. You just join up the dots and see what happens. Then if you like you can colour the picture that comes out. Well, enjoy yourself Cobra.

start here ➔

COBRA'S PUZZLE COMPETITION.

EXAMPLE

Red Wing.

The name of a Bird.

1.

The name of an Insect.

2.

The name of a Bird

3.

The name of a Bird.

Please do not put your answers in the squares, as I have don...

GIRAFFE.

ELEPHANT

Man

Chimpanzee

Dog

Crocodile

Cat

Horse

2.

3.

4.

One day, curious Jane wondered
where eggs came from.

So she and Jubilee snuck into
Grandma Nutt's chicken coop…

hid behind some straw,
stayed very still...

and observed the miracle.

It was a magical world
full of joy and wonder,
and Jane felt very much
a part of it.

Jane often climbed her favorite tree,
which she named Beech.

She would lay her cheek against its trunk
and seem to feel the sap
flowing beneath the bark.

Jane could feel her own heart

beating,

beating,

beating.

With the wind in her hair, she read and reread
the books about Tarzan of the Apes,
in which another girl, also named Jane,
lived in the jungles of Africa.

Jane dreamed of a life in Africa, too...

a life living with,
and helping,
all animals.

At night Jane would tuck Jubilee into bed,
say her prayers,

and fall asleep...

to awake one day…

to her dream come true.

About Jane Goodall

When Jane Goodall was ten years old, she decided that when she grew up she would go to Africa, live with the animals, and write about them. Almost everyone told her this goal was impossible. Her family had little money, and she was a girl in a time when girls were not encouraged to pursue adventurous careers. But her mother encouraged her to follow her dream. When Jane finished school, she continued to learn about Africa and work   save enough money to go there. She finally arrived in 1957, met famed anthropo   us Leakey, and began studying chimpanzees at the Gombe Stream Game Reserve (now known as Gombe Stream National Park) in Tanzania in 1960.

One of Jane's most important observations was her discovery that chimpanzees are able to make and use tools. Until this time, experts thought only humans were able to do so. But based on Jane's remarkable studies, the world was forced to rethink what makes humans different from animals. She wrote about these discoveries and countless other observations in her 1986 book, *The Chimpanzees of Gombe: Patterns of Behavior.*

Today Jane travels around the world raising awareness about the plight of chimpanzees and environmental conservation. Human populations are growing; the forests in Africa where chimpanzees live are being cut down, and chimps and other animals are being hunted for food. She set up the Jane Goodall Institute (JGI), an organization that helps communities near wild places grow more food, have clean water, and send children to school, while also teaching people how to protect the nearby wildlife.

Jane Goodall's Roots & Shoots program has been set up to educate young people everywhere about the world's environmental and social problems and empower them to take action. This growing organization operates in more than 120 countries, and there are tens of thousands of members ranging in age from preschoolers to university students. Learn more at **www.rootsandshoots.org** and **www.janegoodall.org**.

A Message from Jane

Each one of us makes a difference. We cannot live through a single day without making an impact on the world around us — and we have a choice as to what sort of difference we make. The life of each one of us matters in the scheme of things, and I encourage everyone, especially young people, to make the world a better place for people, animals, and the environment.

Children are motivated when they can see the positive results their hard work can have. As I travel, I meet hundreds of Roots & Shoots groups. They are always eager to tell "Dr. Jane" what they've been doing and how they are making a difference in their communities. Whether they've done something simple, like recycling or collecting trash, or something that requires a great deal of effort, like restoring a wetland or raising money for street children or a local dog shelter, they are a continual source of inspiration for me and for other children around the world. I invite you to get involved!

Jane

Jane Goodall, PhD, DBE
Founder — the Jane Goodall Institute
and a United Nations Messenger of Peace

Art Notes

This page features a cartoon that Jane Goodall made of her life in the forest at the Gombe Stream Game Reserve. Readers will also find two facing pages of drawings and puzzles that Jane herself created when, as a young girl, she led a club called the Alligator Society. Throughout the book, ornamental engravings from the nineteenth and early twentieth centuries are included, collectively evoking Jane's lifelong passion for detailed, scientific observation of nature.